DK

DINOSAUR CLUB

Tracking the Diplodocus

Stone

Forshaw

Jamie has just moved to Ammonite Bay, a
stretch of coastline famed for its fossils. Jamie is
a member of Dinosaur Club – a network of
kids who share dinosaur knowledge, help identify
fossils, post new discoveries, and chat about
all things prehistoric. Jamie carries his tablet
everywhere in case he needs to contact the Club.

Jamie is exploring Ammonite Bay when he
meets Tess, another member of Dinosaur Club.
Tess takes Jamie to a cave with a strange tunnel
and some dinosaur footprints. When they walk
along the footprints, the two new friends find
themselves back in the time of the dinosaurs!

It's amazing, but dangerous too – and they'll
definitely need help from Dinosaur Club…

CONTENTS

CHAPTER 1

'Where are you, Grandad?' Jamie
Morgan's voice echoed round the dinosaur
museum on the ground floor of the
lighthouse. 'We're off to hunt for dinosaurs!'

'He'll think we mean fossil dinosaurs,
not real ones,' Tess whispered. The two
friends grinned at one another. Ammonite
Bay had an amazing secret – a cave that
led to a world of real live dinosaurs! Jamie

und Tess had only shared the secret with their friends in Dinosaur Club, a network of kids from around the world who loved everything from prehistory.

'Grandad?' Jamie called again. As he slung his backpack over his shoulders and stepped into the lobby of the museum, his feet scrunched on something gritty.

'What's with these sceds all over the floor?' Tess wondered. 'Maybe he's gardening?'

They hurried out of the front door and looked around the cliff top. There was no sign of Jamie's grandad.

There was a flash of yellow as a little bird with a red head swooped down and began to peck at something on a flat rock beside a bush.

'Look,' Tess said, pointing to the trail
of seeds that led to the rock where the
bird was feasting. The branches of the
bush rustled.

'Grandad?' Jamie called, making the
bird fly off.

'Shhhhh!' hissed the bush.

Jamie laughed in surprise as his grandad emerged from the leaves.

'What are you doing in a bush, Commander Morgan?' Tess asked, as she and Jamie ran over. Jamie's grandad ran the coastguard at Ammonite Bay.

'This is my bird hide,' Commander Morgan whispered. 'I'm taking part in a survey, recording all the different birds that visit Ammonite Bay. That was a goldfinch.'

'Sorry, we scared it away,' Tess said apologetically.

'It'll come back to the birdseed.' Commander Morgan's eyes twinkled. 'It can't resist the bait. Why don't you two try a spot of bird watching?'

'Awesome idea! We know just the place to do it.' Jamie nudged Tess.

Grandad held up his finger. 'Remember, the secret of bird watching is to stay quiet and hidden.' He ducked back into the bush.

'See you later, Grandad!' Jamie called.

They raced off along the path towards Smugglers' Cave.

'Got the ammonite?' Jamie asked.

Tess patted her pocket. 'The Jurassic one,' she confirmed as they reached the cave. The spiral fossil was the key to which time period they would visit.

Jamie took out his torch and they squeezed through the tiny gap at the back of the cave into the secret chamber that lead to Dino World. His heart was thumping with excitement as he placed his feet over the fossil footprints. He took a deep breath and stepped towards the cave wall. 'One, two, three, four... FIVE!'

A crack of light appeared in the solid rock and suddenly he was in the sweltering sunlight of Dino World. His ears filled with the sounds of insects buzzing and the strange calls of unseen creatures out there in the Jurassic jungle.

There was a squelch as Tess trod on
the slimy leaf mould beside him, stirring
up a familiar smell in the hot humid air.

'Phew!' Tess gagged. 'The ginkgo
fruit must be ripe. They're even stinkier
than usual!'

'Wanna will love them!' Jamie pulled
a face.

At the mention of his name, a little
two-legged dinosaur with a very bony
head bounded up to the kids, wagging his
tail, and making happy grunking noises.

'He's pleased to see us!' Tess laughed.
'It's good to see you again, Wanna.'

Wanna looked up hopefully at the
fruit-laden ginkgo tree.

'I'll get you one.' Jamie wrinkled his nose and reached out for an apricot-sized fruit on a nearby branch. It was so ripe that sticky ginkgo goo squished through his fingers. He tried to toss the fruit to the little dinosaur but it stuck fast to his hand.

'Yuck!' Jamie held out his hand. Wanna chomped down the fruit, sticky juice and dino drool trickling onto Jamie's fingers.

'Gross!' Jamie wiped his hand on his jeans.

'Since Wanna's so mad about ginkgoes,' Tess said thoughtfully, 'Maybe we should take some along to bait flying reptiles, like birdseed.'

'We'll be the very first Jurassic birdwatchers!' Jamie filled a plastic

specimen bag with the foul-smelling
fruit and stuffed it in his backpack. He
held out his hands for Wanna to clean.
'Let's go dino bird watching!'

CHAPTER 2

Tess and Jamie plunged into the steamy
Jurassic jungle, and began to wade through
the sea of ferns beneath the tall conifer
trees. Wanna followed them closely, with
his eyes firmly fixed on Jamie's backpack.

Tess got out her binoculars and
looked up.

'What is it?' Jamie asked,
pushing a fern out of his face.

'I can't see anything,' Tess complained as another fern twanged to and fro in front of her lenses. 'We need to find a gap in the jungle.'

They pressed on through the thick undergrowth until they came to a clearing scattered with enormous flat rocks.

'This looks like a good place for bird watching,' Tess said. 'Where shall we hide?'

Jamie looked round. 'How about up there?' He pointed to a tall tree on the edge of the clearing. It was draped with thick rope-like vines. Half way up, two sturdy branches emerged from the trunk together, making a safe platform to sit on.

'Looks good,' Tess agreed, 'but the birds might see us.'

'Not if we make a dino-bird hide!' Jamie said excitedly.

'Cool.' Tess grinned. 'Like a tree house.'

'We can use ferns for the roof and sides...' Jamie grabbed hold of the thick stem of a fern and pulled with all his might. 'I can't pull it up,' he panted, 'it's too tough!'

As he spoke, the fern gave way with a sudden pop and he fell backwards into the soggy leaf mould. He stood up covered in mud, with pine needles and bits of dead fern sticking all over him.

'I look like a swamp monster,' he spluttered.

Tess laughed. 'But it's awesome camouflage! A bit more and you'll look like part of the jungle.' She grabbed a handful of tender fern tips and stuffed them down the neck of Jamie's T shirt.

'I'll get you for that!' Jamie
scooped up an armful of soft mud and
leaf mould and hurled it towards Tess.

Tess stepped sideways and the
muck hit Wanna.

Splat!

'Missed me!' Tess burst into laughter at the sight of the muck-covered dinosaur. Wanna didn't seem to like that. He wagged his tail and lowered his head.

'Go, Wanna, go!' Jamie cheered as Wanna gently barged Tess into the muddy ooze. Jamie rushed over and stuffed some fern tips down his friend's neck.

'Now you're camouflaged too!' They both bent double laughing.

After a moment, Tess struggled to her feet. 'We'll scare away the wildlife with all this noise. Let's get on with making the hide.'

The friends both gathered an armful of dead leaves, then climbed the tree and began weaving them through the dangling vines to make the sides of the hide.

Down below, Wanna put his head on one side and watched curiously. Then he sighed deeply and curled up in the ferns.

'Wanna's taking a nap,' Jamie whispered, peering down at the little dinosaur though a gap in the fern wall.

'That's good,' Tess said, laying the last of the ferns across the top of the hide to make a roof. 'Let's hope he stays still and quiet.'

Jamie took out his tablet and wrote *Dino bird survey* at the top of the screen. Tess smiled, then they peered out through the fern wall into the clearing, watching and waiting.

After a few minutes, something flapped onto the branch of the tree above them.

Through a gap in the fern roof, Jamie

could see the claws in the middle of the
creature's wings gripping onto the trunk.
It looked like an over-grown woodpecker
with electric blue feathers.

'Archaeopteryx,' he breathed.

'Awesome,' Tess whispered, looking through her binoculars. 'Its beak's full of razor-sharp teeth. Take a look.'

As Tess handed Jamie the binoculars, the fern tips sticking out of Jamie's T-shirt tickled his nose. 'A...a...a choo!' he sneezed.

The archaeopteryx took off in an explosion of twigs. Something white and slimy splattered on the fern roof of the hide and dripped down, narrowly missing Jamie's shoulder.

'Yurgh!' Tess grimaced. 'Archaeopteryx poo!

Jamie smiled and opened his tablet on the dino bird survey page. He wrote 'Archaeopteryx' and used a drawing tool to sketch a picture of the creature. Jamie hoped the next entry would be something new and even more exciting.

'Let's put out some ginkgos,' Tess whispered, taking the specimen bag out of Jamie's backpack.

'Don't wake Wanna,' Jamie warned

him. 'Or he'll eat them all.'

As quietly as he could, Tess stretched up her arm and squished a ginkgo fruit onto a branch, sticking it down.

'Let's see what takes the bait,' she whispered.

They sat peering through the gaps in the ferns, waiting for the dino birds.

Nothing came. Jamie shifted uncomfortably on the branch. It was hard sitting still and waiting, but they were determined. Tess got out the tablet to pass the time. She opened the DinoData app and tapped in *Jurassic flying reptiles*. 'My favourite flier's the dimorphodon,' she told Jamie. 'It has a beak like a puffin. It lived much earlier in the Jurassic, though, so we won't see one.'

'Shh,' Jamie whispered.

Just then, the branches of the conifer rustled as a dark orange pterosaur with a wingspan as wide as Jamie's outstretched arms landed on the branch. Its long thin tail with a kite-shaped tip dangled in front of their noses.

'That's a rhamphorhynchus,' Jamie whispered excitedly. Tess passed him the tablet and he added it to his dino bird survey.

Tess focused her binoculars on the flying reptile's long thin jaws. 'Its teeth criss-cross,' she said in surprise.

Jamie held out his hand for the binoculars.

Thunk!

The tree trunk wobbled and Jamie only just managed to hang on to the binoculars. Beneath them, Wanna was standing back from the tree. He lowered his head and barged his head into the tree.

Thunk!

The tree wobbled again. The rhamphorhynchus launched itself into the air with a squawk.

'Stop it, Wanna!' Tess called down. 'You'll scare everything away.'

'He must be bored,' Jamie said. 'A few ginkgos will keep him quiet.' He dropped a stinky fruit that splattered at Wanna's feet. But the little dinosaur took no notice. He head-butted the tree again.

Tess and Jamie looked at each other.

'I don't believe it.' Jamie gasped.

'Wanna NEVER ignores ginkgoes.'

'Something's wrong,' Tess
said nervously.

The tree shook.

'That wasn't Wanna,' Tess gulped.

'Wanna's trying to warn us.

Something's coming!'

CHAPTER 3

A humongous dappled-green, horse-shaped head burst through the front wall of their fern hide, tearing it clean away.

'Get down!' Jamie shouted as the creature swept off the flimsy roof and opened its toothy jaws.

The friends flattened themselves on the floor of the hide.

The tree shook as the long-necked dinosaur stripped the vines from the branch above them.

Tess gulped. 'What is it?'

The gigantic beast grabbed hold of another branch and raked off the pine needles, chewing the greenery with its peg-like teeth.

Jamie heaved a sigh of relief. 'It's a plant eater. But which one?'

He pulled out his tablet, snapped a photo and sent it to the Dinosaur Club.

What is this?

Several messages from their friends came back at once.

A diplodocus! It eats tons of vegetation a day to fuel its huge body, but doesn't stop to chew.

It swallows stones to grind up its food.

Cool, it's an eating machine!

'Thanks guys!'

He stashed the tablet in his backpack as the diplodocus' nose swept away the rest of the fern hide. It sniffed deeply and moved towards Jamie. Its long neck and head were covered in giraffe-like markings in shades of jungle green.

'Stand still,' Tess hissed. 'It wants to eat your ferns, not you!'

The dinosaur's rubbery lips nuzzled at the fresh fern tips sticking out of the neck of Jamie's T shirt.

'It tickles!' Jamie giggled as the huge dino nibbled at the leaves. Below them, Wanna had settled down, realizing that they weren't in danger.

Tess pulled the fern leaves out of the back of her shirt and held them out on the palm of her hand. 'Here you are.'

The gigantic beast took them gently and gulped them down.

'It's like feeding a huge horse,' Tess whispered.

They watched as the diplodocus stripped more branches of pine needles

and swallowed some of the smaller twigs
whole, leaving bare branches draped
with dinosaur drool.

'This tree would make better dino
toothpicks than lunch,' Jamie commented.

'There are some younger creepers
and branches at the top, Dippy,' Tess said.
'Those would be tastier.'

As if he'd heard, the huge dino reared up on his hind legs.

'Awesome!' Jamie murmured. They could see the diplodocus's pale yellow tummy as its elephant-like front legs pawed the air. It stretched out its long neck to grab the thickest branch at the top of the tree. The branch bent, but instead of raking off the leaves and the creepers, the dinosaur hung onto it. The whole tree began to bend and shake.

'Dippy! Let go of the branch,' Tess shouted, hugging the shuddering tree.

There was a craaack as the branch broke off and a thump as the diplodocus's feet hit the ground. The tree swayed back and forth, but the kids managed to cling to their branch.

'Phew!' Jamie breathed.

Beneath them, they could see the diplodocus tearing leaves and twigs from the branches, and gulping them down. Suddenly, the dinosaur's eyes bulged and he swung his head up and began to shake it violently from side to side, making frantic sucking sounds with his tongue.

'What's happening now?' Tess looked worried.

'I'm not sure,' Jamie replied, 'but it doesn't look good.'

The dinosaur's movements became even more erratic and the two friends worried about Wanna getting trampled on the ground.

'Dippy's freaking out!' Tess yelled. 'Let's get out of here before he knocks us off.'

But before they could scramble down the tree, the diplodocus started to bellow, rearing up on his hind legs and thrashing his front feet.

'Hang on,' Jamie yelled as two huge dinosaur feet flailed at the tree.

The tree bent and sprang back, catapulting Tess off the branch. Jamie watched helplessly as his friend fell, clawing wildly at the air. Luckily, she landed on the diplodocus's neck, wrapping her arms around it to stop herself falling further.

'I meant hang onto the tree, not the dinosaur!' Jamie yelled as the diplodocus stomped into the jungle with Tess swinging from its long neck.

CHAPTER 4

From his tree, Jamie could see the diplodocus shaking his head wildly from side to side. Any minute now, Tess would fall off or be crushed against a tree trunk. He had to save his friend!

The end of a thick creeper dangled before his eyes. Jamie took a deep breath, grabbed onto the vine and launched himself towards the next tree. He swung safely across to a thick branch with more vines hanging down. He took hold and leapt off, swinging from tree to tree through the jungle after Tess.

Beneath him, Wanna was leaping logs and dodging branches in his struggle to keep up.

'Yee-haw!' Jamie called as he swung, and soon he was alongside the lumbering diplodocus. Tess was just below the dinosaur's head, and was clinging on for dear life.

'Help!' Tess shouted at the top of her lungs. 'I can't hold on much longer!'

'I'll get you,' Jamie shouted back. He launched himself onto another vine and swung across the diplodocus's path. 'Grab my hand!'

Their fingertips brushed as Jamie swung past the dinosaur's eyes, but he wasn't close enough to reach Tess.

The diplodocus stopped thrashing his head and looked in surprise as Jamie swung back onto the tree.

'I'm coming again!' Jamie took a deep breath and launched himself from the same vine. He swung towards Tess, rising higher and higher, right above the dino's head! At the top of the swing, he stretched his hand down to Tess.

Tess reached up, and they interlocked their fingers.

Jamie had done it!

Snap! The vine gave way.

Jamie plummeted down, and was only saved by his friend's firm grip. While Tess held onto the diplodocus's neck with all her might, Jamie pulled himself up towards the giant reptile's scaly head and clawed for a handhold. He grabbed what felt like a slimy rubbery ledge. He was dangling from the diplodocus's spitty bottom lip!

Whoooooooo!

The diplodocus dropped his head and Jamie quickly let go and tumbled to the ground. Tess landed in a heap beside him.

As the diplodocus pulled away, Jamie could see a piece of wood the size of a baseball bat lodged between the dinosaur's brown teeth and rubbery gums.

'That was awesome!' Tess gasped, checking that her binoculars were in one piece. 'I've never swung from a dinosaur before.'

'First time for me, too,' Jamie panted, trying to catch his breath as he untangled himself from his backpack.

Wanna hurtled out of the jungle and leapt on them, grunking enthusiastically.

'Get off, we're okay!' Jamie struggled to his feet.

Whoooooo!

The diplodocus was wailing again, scraping his jaws along the ground. Then he lifted his head and shook it from side to side.

'I know what's making him so crazy,' Jamie told Tess. 'I saw a piece of tree branch stuck between his teeth.'

As they watched the huge dinosaur stomp off again, Tess said, 'Poor Dippy's got toothache.'

Jamie nodded. 'I had toothache once and it really hurt.'

'We need a dinosaur dentist,' Tess said, 'but we can't just call one up.'

They looked at each other
and grinned.

'Let's go after him,' Jamie said.

Tess nodded. 'We'll be
Dippy's dentists!'

CHAPTER 5

'Follow Dippy's trail!' Tess set off in the direction of a series of circular dents in the leaf mould on the jungle floor.

Wanna dashed ahead and stopped at a mound of slimy orange mush, bobbing his head up and down.

'Dippy's so heavy he mashed that fungus,' Jamie commented.

'And these ferns,' Tess pointed
out a heap of crushed fronds.

Something wet and slimy
splattered down Jamie's neck.
Slimy strings of frothy saliva were
dripping from the tree he was
walking under.

'Dino drool,' he told Tess.
'Dippy must have scraped his
mouth against the branch to
try and get that splinter
out of his jaw.'

The trail led them
to a part of the jungle
crisscrossed with
pathways and
dinosaur footprints.

'Other diplodocus are using these paths,' Jamie said in dismay. 'I can't make out Dippy's trail.'

The two friends scanned the jungle.

'I think he went this way.' Tess set off along a well-trodden jungle path, but Wanna grabbed her sleeve and dug his toes into the ground.

Jamie laughed. 'I think Wanna thinks you're going the wrong way.'

Wanna let go of Tess and then set off
at a brisk trot down another pathway.

They chased after Wanna and soon
burst into a clearing scattered with
enormous flat rocks.

'We're back where we started!' Jamie
exclaimed. 'We've gone round in a circle.'

'There's Dippy.' Tess pointed to the far
side rocks. 'He looks exhausted.'

The huge dinosaur was dragging
his enormous feet and staggering.
As they watched, the diplodocus's legs
buckled and he fell with a humongous

CRASH!

The earth shuddered beneath Tess and
Jamie's feet and there was a moment's
silence in the jungle before the insects

resumed their relentless buzzing.

The diplodocus lay on his side, with his long neck and tail stretched out.

'Oh no,' Jamie said. 'Is he dead?'

'No,' Tess replied. 'His rib cage is moving and there's froth bubbling from his mouth. He's just exhausted. We can still help.'

They hurried towards the collapsed dinosaur. The dinosaur's beady eyes looked at them, but he didn't move. Oily tears oozed from the diplodocus's eyes. He opened his mouth with a pitiful low.

Whoooooooooo.

'We've got to get that splinter out,' Tess said. 'If he's too exhausted to move, the Jurassic scavengers will get him.'

'A real dentist would get it out in no time,' Jamie said.

'He'd never fit in a dentist's chair!' Tess joked. 'We'll have to do it ourselves.'

Jamie and Tess lay on their tummies and wriggled up to the dinosaur's mouth. A blast of warm dino breath and frothy saliva hit them full in the face.

'Yuck!' Jamie gagged. 'His breath smells like rotten eggs.'

'I can't see the branch,' Tess said, wiping the froth away from the diplodocus's jaws. 'We need to get rid of some of this spit.'

Jamie helped, and soon the kids could see the diplodocus's teeth, like two rows of brown tent pegs set in rubbery green

gums. The branch was stuck in his gum between two teeth.

'I think I can get it out.' Jamie gently reached his arm inside the dinosaur's mouth and grabbed the end of the splinter. The diplodocus's mouth felt warm and slimy.

Whoooooooooo.

The gigantic beast moaned but kept still.

'Careful,' Tess breathed.

'Open wide, Dippy.' Jamie tugged at the branch, but his hands only slipped down the wood.

'Do real dentists get covered in this much spit?' Jamie groaned. 'I can't get a good grip.'

'Let me try,' Tess told him.

Jamie wriggled to one side and wiped the dino drool on his jeans while Tess reached in.

'It's much too slimy,' Tess agreed.

The diplodocus closed his eyes as they both sat back on their heels.

'We're not helping – we're just hurting him more,' Tess said with a frown.

Above them came the sound of flapping of wings. Dark grey shapes began to circle like vultures above the exhausted diplodocus.

'Pterosaurs.' Jamie leapt to his feet and shook his fists at them. 'Go away!' he yelled.

Wanna took one look at them and dashed into the jungle.

The sharp-beaked pterosaurs flapped onto the branch of a nearby tree. They stood there, balanced on their feet and the claws of their wings, watching and waiting.

CHAPTER 6

Wanna crept back into the clearing with
a mouthful of soft juicy ferns, and put
them straight into the diplodocus's mouth.

The diplodocus half-heartedly spat
them out.

'It's a good idea to feed him.' Tess
patted Wanna's head. 'But he's in too
much pain to eat.'

'He'll die if we give up on him,' Jamie

said, glancing up at the pterosaurs. 'We have to keep trying. How can we get a better grip on that branch?'

Wanna began hopping from foot to foot, grunking hopefully.

'He wants a ginkgo,' Tess said. 'You'd better give him one or he'll never let us get on with it.'

Jamie got out the specimen bag. All the remaining ginkgo fruit were squashed together in a stinky sticky mess.

'Yuck!' He took out a lumpy handful and scraped it on the ground in front of Wanna. Wanna didn't make a move to eat it – he just looked at Jamie, panting.

Jamie tried to wipe off the foul smelling juice on his T shirt, but it was stuck fast to his hands.

'That's what Wanna was trying to tell us,' Jamie said. 'We can use ginkgo glue!' He took another handful of mushy ginkgoes out of the specimen bag and moved closer to the diplodocus's jaws.

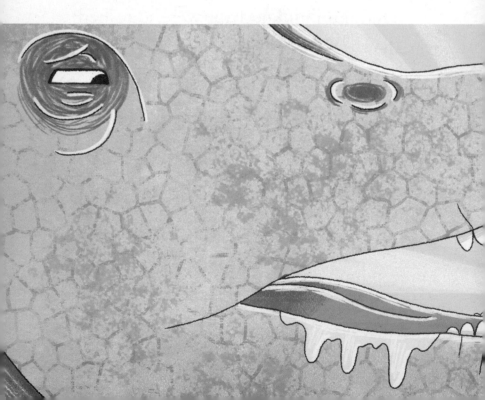

Tess grabbed a handful of ginkgo pulp as well.

Jamie gently mashed the gooey ginkgoes along the branch. 'It's sticking!'

Tess stood beside Jamie and together they started pulling. 'It's moving,' Jamie said. There was a sucking, squelching sound then they fell backwards as the branch came free.

Whooo!

The diplodocus seemed relieved.

The branch was as long as Jamie's arm with a sharp point, covered in mucus. Jamie tossed it into the undergrowth and then watched as Wanna nudged the soft ferns towards the huge dinosaur. The diplodocus gulped them down and gave a contented grunt.

'He's going to be okay.' Jamie and Tess leaped to their feet and shouted out in celebration. The pterosaurs in the tree took off in alarm.

The diplodocus slowly clambered to his feet. Then he gently lowered his head and nuzzled first Tess and Jamie, then Wanna, before turning and lumbering off into the forest.

'We did it!' Jamie grinned, wiping diplodocus drool off his face with the back of his hand. 'We are dino dentists!'

They gave each other a high five. Ginkgo goop spattered down their bare arms.

'Help, Wanna!' Jamie and Tess shouted together, holding out their arms. They cringed as Wanna's sandpapery tongue rasped off every trace of ginkgo juice.

'It's probably time to go,' Jamie said, and they set off for the Cave.

As they came to the clearing in front of it, they saw that the ground was splattered with slimy ripe ginkyoes.

'Who's been eating these?' wondered Jamie, peering up into the ginkgo branches. 'Must be another flying dino!'

But Wanna grunked noisily and started to slurp up the ginkgoes. Jamie and Tess could hear whatever was in the branches flapping away.

Jamie laughed. 'Wanna is terrible at bird watching.'

'He likes the bait too much,' Tess replied with a grin. 'I suppose we've done enough 'bird' watching for one day, anyway. Archaeopteryx, rhamphorhynchus, and those horrible pterosaurs.'

'Definitely,' agreed Jamie. 'See you next time, Wanna!'

The little dinosaur lifted his snout from the ginkgoes and wagged his tail as Jamie and Tess stepped backwards over the footprints. The ground turned to stone beneath their feet and once more, they were back in the secret chamber at the back of Smuggler's Cave.

'Dino dentistry has made me hungry,' Jamie said, as they dashed to the lighthouse.

'Grandad!' he called from the lighthouse door. 'We're back! We're so hungry we could eat a dinosaur.'

'Up here, me hearties,' came the answering cry. Jamie and Tom raced up the stairs to the kitchen.

'I'll make some of my cheese and spicy chilli chutney sandwiches,' Commander Morgan told them with a grin. 'They'll only take a couple of minutes.'

'I can't wait that long.' Jamie spotted a bowl of nuts on the worktop. He put a handful in his mouth and bit down.

'Owwwww! My tooth!' he yelled.

'You're making more noise than a dinosaur at the dentist,' Tess told him.

Jamie spluttered. 'Not as much noise as someone swinging from the neck of a diplodocus.'

'I wish I had your imaginations.' Grandad laughed as he cut up the sandwiches. 'You sound as if you've had a fun day.'

Jamie and Tess grinned
at each other.

'We always have fun
in Ammonite Bay!'

Dinosaur timeline

The Triassic
(250-200 million years ago)

The first period of the Mesozoic Era was the Triassic. During the Triassic, there were very few plants, and the Earth was hot and dry, like a desert. Most of the dinosaurs that lived during the Triassic were small.

The Jurassic
(200-145 million years ago)

The second period of the Mesozoic Era was the Jurassic. During the Jurassic, the Earth became cooler and wetter, which caused lots of plants to grow. This created lots of food for dinosaurs that helped them grow big and thrive.

The Cretaceous
(145-66 million years ago)

The third and final period of the Mesozoic Era was the Cretaceous. During the Cretaceous, dinosaurs were at their peak and dominated the Earth, but at the end most of them suddenly became extinct.

Dinosaurs existed during a time on Earth known us the Mesozoic Era. It lasted for more than 180 million years, and was split into three different periods: the Triassic, Jurassic, and the Cretaceous.

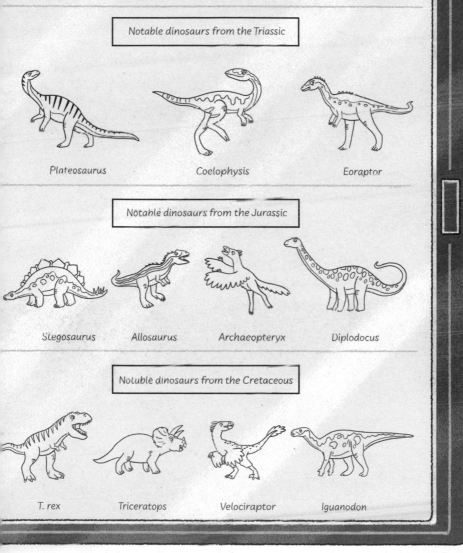

Notable dinosaurs from the Triassic

Plateosaurus

Coelophysis

Eoraptor

Notable dinosaurs from the Jurassic

Stegosaurus

Allosaurus

Archaeopteryx

Diplodocus

Notable dinosaurs from the Cretaceous

T. rex

Triceratops

Velociraptor

Iguanodon

DINO DATA

At about the same length as a blue whale, this sauropod was one of the longest land animals ever to have existed.

Extremely long tail

Spiky plates

FACT

Diplodocus probably used its long tail like a whip to defend itself from attackers.

Name: Diplodocus

Pronunciation: dip-LOD-oh-kus

Period: Jurassic

Size: 25m (82ft) long

Habitat: Plains

Diet: Leaves

Small head

Long neck

FACT

Diplodocus had a row
of spiky triangular
plates running along
the length of its neck,
back, and tail.

DINO DATA

Rhamphorhynchus was a pterosaur from the late Jurassic that lived near coasts and rivers. It soared above the water and swooped down to catch fish.

Name: Rhamphorhynchus
Pronounciation: ram-foe-RINK-us
Period: Jurassic
Size: 1.5m (4ft) wingspan
Habitat: Coasts and rivers
Diet: Fish

Long, narrow jaws

Needle-like teeth

The diamond-shaped
flap of skin at the
end of its tail helped
rhamphorhynchus
steer while flying.

Long wings

FACT

It's likely that rhamphorhynchus
used its needle-like teeth to spear and
catch fish, but some experts believe
they swallowed them whole.

DINO DATA

This pterosaur from the early Jurassic period is known for having two distinct types of teeth. In fact, "dimorphodon" means "Two-form tooth".

Diamond-shape flap of skin

Long bony tail

Name: Dimorphodon
Pronounciation: die-MOR-foe-don
Period: Jurassic
Size: 1m (3ft) wingspan
Habitat: Coasts
Diet: Fish and small animals

FACT

Scientists believe dimorphodon was a clumsy walker and flyer. It's likely it perched in trees and on cliffs.

FACT

Dimorphodon had a head that was about a third of its total body length.

Large head

Long top teeth

QUIZ

1   What was Jamie's grandad doing when the kids found him?

2   True or false: Dimorphodon means "big head".

3   What object became stuck in the diplodocus' teeth?

4   True or false: Diplodocus was a type of sauropod.

5   What did diplodocus use its long whip-like tail for?

6   True or false: Rhamphorhynchus
      lived near rivers and coasts.

CHECK YOUR ANSWERS on page 95

GLOSSARY

AMMONITE
A type of sea creature that lived during the time of the dinosaurs

CARNIVORE
An animal that only eats meat

DINOSAUR
A group of ancient reptiles that lived millions of years ago

FOSSIL
Remains of a living thing that have become preserved over time

GINKGO
A type of tree that dates back millions of years

HERBIVORE
An animal that only eats plant matter

JURASSIC
The second period of the time dinosaurs existed (200–145 million years ago)

PALAEONTOLOGIST
A scientist who studies dinosaurs and other fossils

PTEROSAUR
Ancient flying reptiles that existed at the same time as dinosaurs

PREDATOR
An animal that hunts other animals for food

QUIZ ANSWERS
1. Bird watching
2. False
3. A branch
4. True
5. Defence
6. True

Text for DK by Working Partners Ltd
9 Kingsway, London WC2B 6XF
With special thanks to Jane Clarke

For Andy and Rob, with love

Design by Collaborate Ltd
Illustrator Louise Forshaw
Consultant Dougal Dixon

Acquisitions Editor James Mitchem
Senior Designer and Jacket Designer Elle Ward
Publishing Coordinator Issy Walsh
Production Editor Dragana Puvavic
Production Controller John Casey
Publishing Director Sarah Larter

First published in Great Britain in 2022 by
Dorling Kindersley Limited
One Embassy Gardens, 8 Viaduct Gardens,
London, SW11 7AY

Text copyright © Working Partners Ltd 2008
Copyright in the layouts, design, and illustrations
of the Work shall be vested in the Publishers.
A Penguin Random House Company
10 9 8 7 6 5 4 3 2 1
001-327033-Aug/2022

A CIP catalogue record for this book
is available from the British Library.
ISBN: 978-0-2415-3870-8

Printed and bound in Great Britain by
Clays Ltd, Elcograf S.p.A.

www.dk.com
For the curious

The publisher would like to thank Lynne Murray for picture library assistance.

This book was made with Forest Stewardship Council ™
certified paper – one small step in DK's commitment
to a sustainable future. For more information go to
www.dk.com/our-green-pledge